A TALE OF

Two Pandas

First published 2000 by Happy Cat Books,
Bradfield, Essex CO11 2UT

Printed in Hong Kong by Wing King Tong Co. Ltd.

A TALE OF
Two Pandas

Text by Linda Jennings
Illustrated by Adrienne Kennaway

Happy Cat
Books

Chi Chi woke up, feeling hungry. She had eaten the last
piece of juicy bamboo shoot for supper, and now she
couldn't find any fresh ones. Everything she tried
to chomp looked yellow and tasted horrible.
"I'll go to find Ming," she thought.
"He'll know what to do."

Chi Chi found Ming the red panda staring at the dead
bamboo shoots. "These are no good, Chi Chi," said Ming.
"These are quite rotten. Nothing else you would like
to eat, is there? A nice juicy beetle, perhaps?"
"Ugh," said Chi Chi, shuddering.
Pandas don't like eating anything but bamboo shoots.
"I suppose we'd better look somewhere else," said Ming.
"But where?" asked Chi Chi.

"Let's ask the ibis," said Ming. The big bird always perched on the very top of a tall tree and could see everything for miles around. When Chi Chi and Ming told him about the mouldy bamboo, he looked at them sadly. "Those are the shoots that die after the bamboo has flowered. Eventually new shoots will grow back." "But they've never done this before," said Chi Chi. "That's because the bamboo forest flowers very rarely. I'm afraid you'll have to cross the mountains to find fresh bamboo. Then you follow the golden monkeys through the forest."

"I'm too hungry for such a long journey," grumbled Chi Chi,
but they both knew they would have to find fresh bamboo
somewhere or they would starve to death.
They set off wearily.
They crossed streams and plodded
across grassy meadows.

At last, after lots
of slipping...

and sliding...

and scrambling...

and climbing...

they reached
a big forest
on the other side
of the mountain.

Everything was very quiet under the trees -
until suddenly the two pandas
heard a very strange sound.
"WU, WU, WU!"
"Look! It's the golden monkeys," said Ming.
"Hurry up, or they'll be gone."

The two pandas ran along a track under the tall trees,
as they tried to follow the golden monkeys. But the
monkeys were going too fast for Ming and Chi Chi.
Very soon all they could hear were their distant cries,
"WU, WU, WU, wu..."
Then there was silence.
The golden monkeys had disappeared.

"We'll never find the bamboo forest now!" wailed Chi Chi.
"There's no one to ask."
"Hey, what's that?" asked Chi Chi, staring.
A big bulky, hairy animal was lying on the
path in front of them.
"Get right down, and keep still !" it hissed at them.

The hairy animal was a takin. Takins always flatten
themselves on the ground when there's danger about.
The two trembling pandas crouched down
beside him, still as statues.
"Look, there it is," whispered the takin.
A very large leopard was sneaking up on
a pheasant, ready to pounce...

...but the pheasant was too quick for him.
She fluttered from tree to tree, as the frustrated leopard
tried to catch her. Very softly, Takin, Chi Chi and Ming
crept out of the forest. "That was close!" said the takin,
getting to his feet. "I must say I feel quite hungry now.
Would you like something to eat?"
"That's very kind of you to ask," said Ming politely,
"but you see, pandas don't eat just anything.
They only like ... "

" ... bamboo shoots!" said the takin. "Yes, I know.
That's why I've invited you!
Take a look behind those rocks."
The two pandas clambered over the rocks.
They stared and stared,
because there in front of them...

...was a huge bamboo forest -
enough bamboo to last them a lifetime!
Chi Chi and Ming and the takin ate
and ate until they were completely full.
It was the best meal they'd ever had.
And all around them the golden monkeys swung
through the trees. "WU, WU, WU!" they went.
"WU, WU, WU!"